The Best Town in the World

By Byrd Baylor   Pictures by Ronald Himler

Aladdin Books

Macmillan Publishing Company / New York

For George Baylor's great-grandchildren
Ruby, Ian, Seth, Claire, Leah, Sarah, and Jesse

Text copyright © 1982 by Byrd Baylor
Illustrations copyright © 1983 by Ronald Himler

Aladdin Books
Macmillan Publishing Company
866 Third Avenue, New York, NY 10022
Collier Macmillan Canada, Inc.

First Aladdin Books edition 1986
Printed in the United States of America
A hardcover edition of *The Best Town in the World* is available from
Charles Scribner's Sons, Macmillan Publishing Company.
10 9 8 7 6 5 4 3 2

Library of Congress Cataloging-in-Publication Data
Baylor, Byrd. The best town in the world.
Summary: A nostalgic view of the best town in the
world, where dogs were smarter, chickens laid prettier
brown eggs, wildflowers grew taller and thicker, and
the people knew how to make the best chocolate cakes
and toys in the world.
[1. City and town life—Fiction] I. Title.
[PZ7.B3435Bf 1986] [Fic] 86-3381
ISBN 0-689-71086-0 (pbk.)

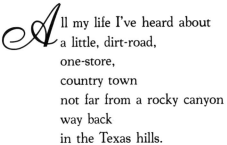

All my life I've heard about
a little, dirt-road,
one-store,
country town
not far from a rocky canyon
way back
in the Texas hills.

This town had lots of space
around it
with caves to find
and honey trees
and giant rocks to climb.

It had a creek
and there were panther tracks
to follow
and you could swing
on the wild grapevines.
My father said it was
the best town in the world
and he just happened
to be born there.
How's that for being
lucky?

We always liked
to hear about
that town
where everything was
perfect.

Of course it had a name
but people called the town
and all the ranches
and the farms around it
just *The Canyon*,
and they called each other
Canyon People.
The way my father said it,
you could tell
it was a special thing
to be
one of those people.

*A*ll the best cooks
in the world lived there.
My father said
if you were walking down the road,
just hunting arrowheads
or maybe coming home from school,
they'd call you in
and give you
sweet potato pie
or gingerbread
and stand there
by the big wood stove
and smile at you
while you were eating.

It was that kind
of town.

The best blackberries
in the world
grew wild.

My father says
the ones in stores
don't taste a thing
like those
he used to pick.
Those tasted just like
a blackberry should.

He'd crawl into
a tangle
of blackberry thicket
and eat all he wanted
and finally
walk home
swinging his bucket
(with enough for four pies)
and his hands
and his face
and his hard bare feet
would be stained
that beautiful color.

All plants
liked
to grow there.
The town was famous for
red chiles
and for melons
and for sweet corn, too.

And it's a well-known fact
that chickens in that canyon
laid prettier brown eggs
than chickens
twenty miles on down the road.

My father says
no scientist
has figured out
why.

The dogs were smarter there.
They helped you herd the goats
and growled at rattlesnakes
before you even saw them.
And if you stopped
to climb a tree
your dogs stopped, too.
They curled up and waited
for you to come down.
They didn't run off
by themselves.

Summer days
were longer there
than they are
in other places,
and wildflowers grew taller
and thicker on the hills—
not just the yellow ones.
There were all shades of
lavender and purple
and orange and red
and blue
and the palest kind of pink.
They all had butterflies
to match.

Fireflies lit up
the whole place
at night,
and in the distance
you could hear
somebody's fiddle
or banjo
or harp.

My father says
no city water
ever tasted half as good
as water that he carried
in a bucket from the well
by their back door.

And there isn't
any water
anywhere
as clear
as the water
in that ice cold creek
where all the children swam.
You could look down
and see the white sand
and watch the minnows
flashing by.

But
when my father came to the part
about that ice cold water
we would always say,

"It doesn't sound
so perfect
if the water was
ice cold."

He'd look surprised
and say,
"But that's the way
creek water
is supposed to be—
ice cold."

So we learned that
however
things were
in that town
is just exactly how
things *ought* to be.

People there
did things
in their own way.
For instance —
spelling.

Sometimes I'd be
surprised
at how my father
spelled a word
that I'd already learned
at school,
but if I mentioned it,
he'd say,
"The way I spell it
is the way
they spelled it
there,
so it must be right."

But my mother said
since we weren't living
there,
maybe we should just
go ahead
and spell the way
they do in other places.
So we did,
though we always liked
his way.

Maybe that's part of the reason
it was the best town
in the world.
You could do things
whatever way
seemed good
to you.

For instance, in the summertime
when the air was full of birdsong
and cicadas,
my father
(when he was little
and even when he was big)
liked to take his supper
and climb up in a tree
and eat it there
alone.

He did it almost every night.
He had thick slices
of his mother's homemade bread
in a bowl of milk,
fresh from the evening milking.

No one ever said,
"Eat something else,"
and no one ever said,
"Don't eat it in a tree."
If someone, walking by,
glanced up and saw him
with his bowl and spoon,
they wouldn't say a thing
except,
"Good evening, George."

Of course you knew
everyone's name
and everyone
knew
yours.

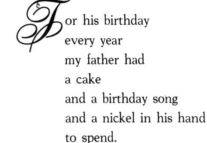For his birthday
every year
my father had
a cake
and a birthday song
and a nickel in his hand
to spend.

He'd jump on his horse,
Doodlebug,
and ride off
as fast as he could,
stirring up dust
all the way
to Mr. Patterson's store.

He always bought
a nickel's worth
of candy.

"It doesn't seem like much,"
we'd say.

He'd say,
"Remember,
this was not just
any candy.
This was the best
in the world."

There was a bin of it.
Sometimes
he'd stand there
half the morning,
choosing
five pieces
while everybody gave him
good advice.

He says
he never did
choose *wrong*.
He still remembers
how that candy
used to taste.

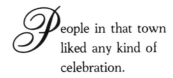People in that town
liked any kind of
celebration.

The best speeches
in the world
were made right there
on Texas Independence Day
and July Fourth.

And every Sunday
people from the farms
and ranches
came to town
with wagons full of children
and baskets full of food.

After church,
the whole town gathered
at long tables
underneath the tall shade trees
where all those famous cooks
were bringing out
their famous food.

You could count on fried chicken
and chile con carne
and black-eyed peas
and corn on the cob
and corn bread sticks
and biscuits
and frijoles
and squash and turnip greens
and watermelon pickles
and dumplings
and fritters
and stews.

There was another whole table
just for desserts.
Sometimes you'd see
five different kinds of
chocolate cake.

My father said
he thought that if
he took just one
he'd hurt the feelings of
four other
chocolate cake cooks—
so he took one
of each.
But then he thought
that if they saw him
eating cake
he'd hurt the feelings of
the pie cooks,
so he ate pie, too—
to be polite.

He said
he was famous
for being polite
to the cooks.

It seemed like
everybody
in that town
was famous.

My father said
it was because
the smartest people
in the world
were
all
right there.

We asked him
what they did
that was so smart.
He said,
"They all had sense enough
to know the best town
in the world
when they saw it.
That's smart."

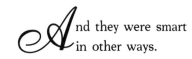nd they were smart
in other ways.

For instance,
they could tell time
without wearing a watch.
They just glanced
at the sun
and they *knew*.
They wouldn't be more
than ten minutes off...
and ten minutes off
doesn't matter.

They could tell
by the stars
what the weather would be.
They could tell
by the moon
when to plant.

If they needed
a house
or corral
or a barn,
they didn't pay someone
to come build it for them.
They cut their own trees
and found their own rocks
and dug their own earth.

Then,
whatever it was,
they built it to last
for a hundred years—
and it did.

Suppose
their children
wanted
kites
or jump ropes
or whistles
or stilts...

They didn't have to
go to stores
and buy just what
was there.

They knew how to make
the best toys
in the world.

On winter nights
when they were
sitting by the fire,
by lamplight,
talking,
you'd see them
making
bows and arrows
or soft rag dolls
or blocks
or tops
or bamboo flutes
or even a checkerboard
carved out of oak.

My father said
sometimes
they'd let you
paint the checkers
red
or black
and you'd be
proud.

We liked everything
we ever heard
about those people
and that town,
but we always
had to ask:
"If it really was
the best town
in the world,
why weren't
more people
there?"

And he would say,
"Because
if a lot
of people
lived there,
it wouldn't be
the best town
anymore.
The best town
can't
be crowded."

We always wished
that we could live there
and be
Canyon People, too.

Still,
we used to wonder
if possibly,
just *possibly*,
there might be
another
perfect town
somewhere.

To find out,
I guess
you'd have to follow
a lot of
dirt roads
past
a whole lot of
wildflower hills.

$\mathcal{I}$ guess
you'd have to
try
a lot of
ice cold
swimming holes
and eat
a lot of
chocolate cake
and pat
a lot of dogs.

It seems
like a good thing
to do.